FLORIZELLA AN

Princess Florizella is a princess with a mind of her own. But when a mountainous giant invades her kingdom, even Florizella finds she has a challenge on her hands!

Philippa Gregory created Princess Florizella for her daughter, "as an antidote to the drippy heroines of fairy tales". Both *Florizella and the Giant* and *Florizella and the Wolves* are available on audio cassette. Philippa Gregory is an internationally acclaimed author of adult fiction, including the bestselling *Wideacre* trilogy and *A Respectable Trade*, which she adapted as an award-winning BBC TV series.

Also by Philippa Gregory

Florizella and the Wolves

Florizella
AND THE
GIANT

Philippa Gregory
Illustrations by
Patrice Aggs

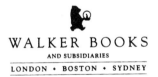

WALKER BOOKS
AND SUBSIDIARIES
LONDON • BOSTON • SYDNEY

For Victoria

First published 1992 by Walker Books Ltd
87 Vauxhall Walk, London SE11 5HJ

This edition published 2000

2 4 6 8 10 9 7 5 3 1

Text © 1992 Philippa Gregory
Illustrations © 1992 Patrice Aggs

This book has been typeset in Sabon.

Printed in England by Clays Ltd, St Ives plc

British Library Cataloguing in Publication Data
A catalogue record for this book is
available from the British Library.

ISBN 0-7445-7258-4

CONTENTS

Chapter 1

What terror there is in the Seven Kingdoms! A giant has arrived. A giant bigger than any giant that has ever been before.

A super-giant. A mega-giant.

An absolutely staggeringly giant giant for which there is only one suitable word –

MOUNTAINOUS.

So say the people of the Plain Green Plains at the south of the Seven Kingdoms and *they* should know because it is *their* plain green fields which the giant tramples every day, and *their* crops which are squashed every time he lies down to take a nap, and *their* houses which are shaken to pieces every time he does a little jog, or a little jig, or a little wriggle; or whatever it is that he is doing up there.

For no one can see whether he is red-faced and running, or smiling and dancing, or yawning and stretching. No one has even seen his head – it is too high. All that anyone has ever seen of him is his huge (super-huge), trampling (mega-trampling) boots.

"I don't believe one word of it," Princess Florizella said to her particular friend, Prince Bennett. They were sitting behind her parents' thrones listening to the messenger from the Plain Green Plains gasping for breath and shaking with fright as he told the king and the queen of the Seven Kingdoms that Something Must Be Done! ("Like what?" Florizella muttered to Bennett.) At Once! ("By whom?" Bennett whispered back.) To save the people of the Plain Green Plains from being squashed

as flat as well-trodden chewing gum by this
ex-tra-ord-in-ar-il-y big giant.

The king looked very worried. "When was
the last time we had a giant?" he asked the
court herald.

She consulted the scroll. "Ages ago, Your
Majesty," she said. "In your father's father's
father's father's time. The young king (your
father's father's father's father) went out and
challenged the giant to single combat and
slew him after three days of bloody battle, in
which he was nearly killed three times over!"

"Well, we don't want any of that I'm sure,"
the king said hastily. "Why don't we just ask
him to move on?"

There was a muffled giggle from Bennett,
still hidden by the big gold throne. "Not into
my kingdom you don't!" he said to Florizella.
"We don't want a giant any more than you
do!"

The messenger from the Plain Green Plains
shook his head. "We have tried asking the
giant to move," he said. "He responds to

nothing. We have shouted at him, and written letters to him. We sent him a petition. We had a demonstration. We had a protest march and a rock concert. He just keeps trampling on our crops and scooping up whole barns of wheat and taking them off. He gathers forests of saplings like a child might pick daisies. He scoops up fishponds in his hand and drinks them dry. Your Majesty *must* save us!"

"Yes," said the king thoughtfully. "I can see that you would think that." He turned to the queen. "Any ideas my love?" he asked.

The queen nodded briskly. "Send the royal surveyor," she said. "He's good at measuring things. He's just come back from mapping the Red Mountains. He can measure the giant for us and estimate how we can move him, and where he should be placed. We need to know a lot more about him before we take any action."

"And send the royal zoo keeper too," the king said. "He might have some idea about capturing him and feeding him."

"And a magician, to be on the safe side," the queen said. "I'd never trust a surveyor without a magician to keep an eye on him."

"An expedition!" the king said cheerfully. "We'll *all* go."

The messenger from the Plain Green Plains dropped to his knees. "I thank Your Majesties!" he said. "I'll ride straight home and tell my people you are coming at once to save them! We will expect you immediately."

"At once!" the king said. He stood up and waved his sceptre with a flourish.

"At once!" everybody said, waving back at him happily.

"It'll take four days for this lot to get packed, never mind started!" said Florizella to Bennett, still hidden behind the thrones. "We'd better get our ponies and leave now, and see this giant before everyone else arrives and spoils everything."

Bennett nodded and the two of them slid very carefully through the curtains at the back of the thrones, out of the hidden door, and then across the hall of the castle to the kitchens. "I'll saddle up the ponies, you get a picnic," said Bennett. "See you at the front gateway in five minutes."

Florizella was a lucky princess for many reasons. She had managed to persuade her parents that she and Bennett would be friends for ever, and that they might never marry. She planned to share her kingdom with everyone who lived in it as soon as she was queen. All the royal gardens would be opened for everyone to walk in them. All the royal palaces would be used as homes for families who had nowhere else to live. All the royal treasure would be used to build hospitals and schools and theatres. Florizella didn't really believe in kings and queens at all – she thought that everyone should be treated the same.

Florizella was not at all pretty, and she did not care. She had decided some time ago that she was not going to be an ordinary, pretty princess in a fairy story – and so she had a lot more fun than ordinary, pretty princesses. For instance, no one had ever tried to kidnap Florizella. It would have been a brave kidnapper who tried to snatch *her*! No dragons had ever tied her up and fought handsome princes for her fair hand. It would have been a super-quick dragon to have got a grip on her in the first place, and a reckless one indeed who tried to bully her like that. And, of course, no one could ever have fought for Florizella's fair hand because her hands were rarely fair. They were more often grubby and sometimes sticky, depending on what she was doing.

She was very brave and very clever – not at all like goody-goody girls in ordinary fairy stories. She was extremely quick when sword-fighting, she was excellent at horse-riding, she could swim underwater with her eyes open, she could climb trees and even small mountains. She was no good at all at French, needlework, dancing, singing in a silvery voice, or Royal Manners. She could have thrown and caught a golden ball if she had wanted to – but she had never tried. She was quite good at football.

And she could pack a *brilliant* picnic.

Into two rucksacks Florizella piled the following:

 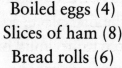 Boiled eggs (4)
Slices of ham (8)
 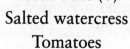 Bread rolls (6)
Salted watercress
Tomatoes
 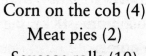 Corn on the cob (4)
Meat pies (2)
Sausage rolls (10)
 Cheese
Crisps

Three packets of those crispy things that look like seashells and are crunchy when you put them in your mouth but then go all deliciously squashy and you have to eat another one. No one in the entire history of the universe has ever eaten only one – unless they were showing-off.

 Peanuts
Salted biscuits
Lemonade (4 bottles)

Bars of chocolate (12)
Chocolate biscuits
Chocolate cake
Chocolate pudding
(Florizella was rather fond of chocolate.)
Popcorn (4 large bags)
Peaches (8)
Strawberries (4 punnets)
Raspberries (8 punnets)
Gooseberries (2 punnets)
Plums
Greengages
Apricots
Apples
(Florizella was rather fond of fruit, too.)

They were rather large and bulky rucksacks once all that was crammed inside, but Florizella thought that you can never take too much food on a serious adventure. You never know how long you will be away from home, and if matters get desperate you can always use it for ammunition.

She dashed upstairs and fetched her best sword from her bedroom, and then ran out of the castle, lugging the rucksacks, to meet Bennett at the gate. As she ran she whistled for her pet wolf cub, Samson, who came lolloping out of the stable yard, his coat very golden in the sunshine. Florizella and Bennett had dyed him blond so that no one knew she had a wolf cub for a pet. Everyone thought that Samson was an extraordinarily yellow Alsatian dog.

The portcullis was up, the drawbridge was down. No one stopped the Prince and Princess and asked them where they were going and if they were allowed; everyone was used to the two of them riding all over the place on their own.

Very soon Bennett and Florizella, mounted on their fine ponies, with Samson loping along behind them, were trotting briskly down the white chalky road which wound far ahead, around the hills and woods, southwards to the Plain Green Plains.

Chapter 2

It is rather an extraordinary experience hunting a giant. You don't need dogs to smell him out, as if you were hunting pheasant or duck. The smell of a giant, even an extremely clean giant, wafts all around him for about ten kilometres in any direction. This particular giant had found a store of onions on the very morning that Florizella and Bennett arrived at the Plain Green Plains and the smell of his breath was enough to knock them off horseback.

"Yuk," said Florizella, clinging to the mane of her brilliant bay pony, Jellybean, while warm gales of onion-scented wind buffeted them.

Samson the wolf let out a short, yappy howl. "Ki-yi-yi-yi-yi!" His nose was burning with too much scent and his eyes were watering.

When hunting a giant you don't need sharp eyesight to pick out his well-camouflaged body – like hunting little deer that can disappear into a forest, or sleek hares that lie low and blend into the ground. This giant blocked the sunlight; his feet and legs, thicker and bigger than tree trunks, towered above the flat fertile lands of the Plain Green Plains. Florizella's pony, Jellybean, and Bennett's pony, Thunderer, stopped dead a good kilometre from the giant boots, and kept a close watch on one giant bootlace, which was undone and snaked across the road as big as a rope to hold a sailing ship. Samson blinked miserably and growled under his breath.

He really was a very big giant indeed. Florizella and Bennett had been privately certain that the messenger from the Plain Green Plains was exaggerating when he had called the giant "mountainous". Their high spirits on the day-long ride had been because they thought they were on their way to a giant perhaps three metres tall. But now they were close to him they could see why the messenger had been so determined that the King himself should come and sort out the problem. The adventure suddenly seemed *very* serious.

Even sitting on their horses, Bennett and Florizella were only just level with the giant's ankles in his thick knitted socks. Standing on the ground, they only came up to his big polished toe-caps. They could not even see his head. His broad legs, dressed in socks and big baggy breeches, and his big tummy, in a green jerkin with a belt, blocked the view upwards like an overhanging balcony on a house.

Florizella and Bennett got off their horses and turned them loose in a nearby field. The horses kicked up their heels and rushed over to the far side and tried, very foolishly, to hide under the hedge. Horses *hate* giants and Jellybean especially disliked Florizella's more dangerous adventures.

"I have a Plan," said Bennett. Bennett often had a Plan.

"We will summon him to a Parley. And then we will issue our challenge to him."

"Challenging him to what?" Florizella asked.

"Single combat with sword and lance,"

Bennett said promptly. "You'll have to fight him, Florizella. It's your kingdom, after all."

"Not me," Florizella said equally promptly. "You must be crazy, Bennett. It would be like a mouse challenging you to single combat. I think we should talk with him. He may be lost. Or just passing through."

"Combat would be more princely," Bennett said regretfully. "But I suppose you're right. How shall we talk to him?"

"We need a white flag," Florizella said. "To show that we want a peaceful talk. Have you got a clean handkerchief?"

Bennett just laughed. Neither of them *ever* had a clean handkerchief.

"We'll use your shirt," Florizella said. "It's white enough under the dirt. And anyway, we're not asking him to check up on the laundry. We just want to attract his attention and show him we mean peace."

Bennett took off his shirt and they tied it to a fallen branch of a tree. Then they went as close to the giant boots as they thought safe and waved the flag in the air.

They waved for a long time.

Nothing happened.

"I don't think he can see us," Florizella said.

"My arms are tired," Bennett said. "Let's shout at him."

The two children bawled upwards. "EXCUSE US! WE WANT TO TALK TO YOU!"

Absolutely nothing happened.

"This is stupid," Florizella said. "We'll have to get him to look down. I'll stab him in the ankle with my sword."

"Better not," Bennett said cautiously. "It might hurt him."

"No," Florizella said. "Look at the thickness of his socks. It would only be like a little mosquito bite."

"Mm," said Bennett. "And what do people do to mosquitoes?"

"Swat them," Florizella said. Then she said, "Oh, I see."

"We have to get him down to our level,
without making him angry," Bennett said
thoughtfully. He was staring at the great rope
of bootlace. Then he snapped his fingers.
"I am a Genius!" he said. "We'll knot his
bootlace to that tree, then he'll notice it has
come undone, and kneel down to do it up.
Then he'll see us, and we can talk to him."

"Great," said Florizella.

The two of them took hold of the rope, and
with much heaving and shoving got it tied
round a sturdy oak
tree which grew
in a little
copse of
other trees
at the side
of the road.

Samson sat down beside the rope and tried to look optimistic. He was a *very* unhappy wolf cub.

"Look out!" Florizella yelled. "He's moving!"

She was right. One giant boot strode forward, the other one, securely fastened to the oak tree, moved a little, the rope strained tight, tight, tighter,
and then...

Pee-yoing!

The rope snapped, the great boot shot forward, stumbled, and with a crash like a thousand earthquakes the mighty giant fell to the earth, crushing two fences and sprawling over four fields.

"Oh brilliant," Florizella said crossly. "Now he's knocked himself out!"

Chapter 3

The two children walked round the giant's head. It was as big as a small hill. His skin was as rugged and as rough as a pebbly beach. His beard was a forest of thick golden hair. The hair on his head was a jungle of curls. He had fallen with his head turned to one side, and he was smiling slightly as if he were having pleasant dreams.

"What shall we do?" Florizella asked Bennett.

"Wait till he wakes up, I suppose," Bennett said. "I hope he won't have a headache," he added, a little nervously. "I think he hit his head as he fell."

"He can't eat us," Florizella said without thinking. Then she said, "Oh! I suppose he *could*."

A small crowd of the Plain Green Plains people had come running when they had heard the great thunder of the falling giant.

"Cut his throat, Florizella!" someone shouted from the back of the crowd. "Before he wakes up."

"Certainly not!" Florizella and Bennett both said at once.

"He's eaten all our food and destroyed hundreds of houses," a woman cried. "He should be punished."

"In the old days the prince would have challenged him to single combat," a man said, looking at Bennett.

"Those days are gone," Bennett said firmly. "Anyway, we don't want to kill him, we just want to move him on somewhere else."

The giant stirred slightly. Everyone in the crowd – especially the people who had talked very boldly about cutting his throat or single combat – rushed backwards and stayed there, nervously watching. Only Florizella and Bennett waited where they were, right in front of the giant's face.

Slowly the giant opened his huge blue eyes.

"Hello," Florizella squeaked. Because she was scared, her voice came out too high. She tried again. "Hello!" she said. This time she sounded like a cow mooing.

"This is the land of Seven Kingdoms," Bennett said as loudly and as clearly as he could. "This is Princess Florizella, princess of this land. I am Prince Bennett of the next door kingdom, the Kingdom of the Blue Hills." He bowed very smartly, then he glanced back at Florizella. "She really *is* a princess," he said. "She looks like a princess when she is clean."

Florizella scowled at Bennett. "I welcome you to my country," she said politely. "Er ... will you be staying long?"

The giant's eyes at once filled with great round pools of tears.

"Unh-hunh," he bellowed.

He was crying, with great loud sobs, so noisy that they were like thunderclaps, roaring one after another. Florizella and Bennett were bowled over by the blast of his breath. They clung to each other on the ground while the onion-scented gale nearly blew them away.

Samson, in the shelter of the trees, tried to rush to Florizella's side but was blown over and over until he stuck in a bush.

"Go up!" Bennet yelled in Florizella's ear. "Up! Away from his mouth!"

The two of them, clinging to bushes and grass, crawled away from the giant's mouth towards his nose.

"Unh-hunh! Unh-hunh! Unh-hunh!"

The giant was sobbing now as if he would never stop. Great fat, round tears as big as boulders rained down on Florizella and Bennett, drenching them with warm salty water as they struggled to get away from the hurricane of the giant's grief.

"Stop crying!" Florizella yelled. "Stop crying!"

"Unh-hunh!"

the giant went, as loud as ever.

"What's the matter?" Bennett shouted.

A huge teardrop splashed to the ground, drenching them both as if someone had thrown buckets of warm water at them.

"I'm hungry! And I'm lost!"

Another thunderstorm of tears poured down upon the children. Another ear-splitting sob nearly blew them away.

"We can't survive much more of this!" Bennett yelled to Florizella. "He must stop!"

Florizella nodded. "Shove me up towards his ear," she said.

Bennett got beneath Florizella and pushed her up, towards the giant's bushy yellow beard, towards the great dark cavern of his ear-hole.

"Don't fall in!" Bennett yelled. "Don't go near the edge."

Florizella nodded and took a firm grip on the silky undergrowth of the giant's beard. "We are your friends," she yelled down the cave of his ear-hole. "We will get you some food. We will help you find your way home. STOP CRYING!"

The giant stopped suddenly. The silence was so startling after the roaring sobs and crashing tears that Bennett shook his head, thinking he had gone deaf.

Samson struggled out of the bushes and sat down sulkily to lick his paws.

"You'll be my friend?"

the giant said. The earth shook slightly. Behind Bennett a tree crashed to the ground.

"You must whisper," Florizella shouted. "You nearly blew us away just now. We are very small. You must whisper to us."

"You'll be my friend?" the giant whispered.

Bennett cautiously sat up.

"Yes!" he yelled. "And we will help you. What are you doing in this country?"

The giant's huge lower lip quivered, his eyes filled with tears.

"He's off again!" Bennett yelled to Florizella. "Watch out!"

"DON'T CRY!" Florizella shouted. "We will help you! There's nothing to cry about!"

"There isn't?" the giant asked.

"NO!" the two children yelled together.

A little smile came across the giant's huge, handsome, moon face. He said:

"I was hungry, I don't have a mother or a father to care for me. I'm an orphan. I live alone and I have to grow my own food."

His lower lip trembled.

"Watch out," Bennett said warningly, getting a good grip around a small tree trunk.

"But I can't read the writing on the seed packets that I bought to plant in my garden. I thought I had planted tomato seeds and lettuce seeds, but all that came up were flowers."

Florizella dropped down from the giant's beard and stood beside Bennett.

"Poppies!" the giant said sadly. "Very pretty. But I was hungry."

"You poor thing," Florizella said comfortingly.

The giant's huge misty blue eyes turned

towards her. He let out a soft sob.

"Don't be nice to him," Bennett said urgently. "You'll set him off again."

"You're very kind." The giant snuffled a little. "Like a friend. I've never had a proper friend."

"Watch out," Bennett said. "Here we go."

"Don't cry!" Florizella yelled. "I would never be friends with a cry-baby."

With a great gulp the giant swallowed his sorrow. "I'll try not," he said humbly. "But I've come an awful long way and I have been very lonely and very hungry. I left my little cottage weeks ago. I walked a long way until I came here. There were lots of things to eat then. But there seems to be less now."

"That's because you've eaten it all," Bennett shouted severely. "Perhaps you should move on."

The giant sat up. The little wood shook as he moved. He put his hand down and the two children climbed into the warm palm.

He lifted them up in the air, high, high, higher, until they were level with his face. He sighed sadly. Bennett and Florizella clung to his thumb until the storm passed.

"But I'm lost," he said sadly. "I can't find my way home now. It's horrible being lost, and hungry, and not knowing your way home."

Florizella and Bennett glanced at each other. "We know the direction you came from," Bennett said. "We could put you on the right road. Would you know your way from the borders of the Seven Kingdoms?" He paused. "Avoiding the Kingdom of the Blue Hills," he suggested. Bennett didn't think his mother and father the king and queen would be too pleased if he directed a huge and hungry giant across their lands.

The giant shook his enormous head. "I don't think so. I couldn't see very well. I just wandered round, but it was all a blur to me. And what shall I do when I get home? There'll be nothing for me to eat. I've got nothing to plant in my garden, and I need the right seeds. Vegetable seeds."

"But if we gave you some vegetable seeds from our gardeners they would grow too small, wouldn't they?" Florizella asked.

"Not in my country," the giant said a little more cheerfully. "As soon as they get into the earth of my country, tomatoes grow as big as your elephants!" He snuffled. "But I can't even see elephants clearly!"

Florizella tugged at Bennett's arm. "D'you think his eyesight is all right?" she whispered. "He couldn't read the seed packets and he couldn't see where he was going. If he can't even see elephants he must be short-sighted!"

"A short-sighted giant would have *real* trouble," Bennett said. "He'd have to be long-sighted just to be able to see his feet."

"Have you ever been able to see things clearly?" Florizella yelled at the giant.

Slowly he shook his big handsome head.

"No. I couldn't see the blackboard at school, or my books. And everybody thought I was stupid."

His big mouth turned down again. "Stupid," he said sadly. "They called me stupid at school."

"We don't think you're stupid," Bennett said quickly. "We like you. We said that we will be your friends. What's your name?"

"Simon," the giant said solemnly. "My name is Simon. I'm very pleased to meet you."

Bennett did his most princely bow. "I'm pleased to meet you, too, Simon," he said kindly. "And we're going to help you. Wait right there and we'll be back in a little while."

The giant lowered his mighty hand to earth again and the children jumped off.

"Don't go away, Simon!" Florizella warned him. "We won't be long. And you don't want to tread on us!"

"Oh, I wouldn't do that! I'll stay still! I love mice."

"Mice?" Florizella asked Bennett. "Did he say mice?"

"Never mind that now," Bennett said quickly. "We've got an awful lot to do. We've got to feed him and get him something to drink. We've got to persuade everyone not to challenge him to combat."

"That won't be too hard!" Florizella said, nodding towards the people of the Plain Green Plains who were still keeping a very safe distance away.

"And we've got to solve all his problems!" Bennett went on.

Florizella stopped dead. "All of them! How?" she asked.

"Spectacles!" Bennett said triumphantly. "We're going to make him a pair of spectacles!"

Chapter 4

Within an hour Bennett had the Seven Kingdoms' Fire Brigade – all twenty-three fire engines – lined up beside the largest lake in the Kingdom, pumping kilos of sugar and litres of lemon juice into it, and then pumping the whole sticky, sweet, glorious lake of lemonade into their enormous tanks.

All the children from the nearest school – Great Valley Lake School – played truant for the whole day and went down to the lakeside with straws and sucked until they were blue in the face from lack of air, and then green in the face from too much lemonade.

Then, with Bennett sitting beside the driver in the cab of the leading fire engine (he had always longed to do that) *and* with the siren going, the complete brigade of twenty-three fire engines went roaring down the road to the Plain Green Plains where the giant was sitting patiently, as still as a rock in the little wood, waiting for Florizella and Bennett to come back.

The firemen unpacked their thickest and

longest hosepipe and held it up to the giant.
Simon put it carefully into his cavernous
mouth, and then they pumped a steady
stream of sweet lemonade up to him,
emptying every one of the twenty-three fire
engines, until at last the giant burped an
earth-shattering burp and said:

"Pardon me."

Meanwhile Florizella, mounted on
Jellybean, with Samson trotting behind her
(very fast away from the giant, rather slowly
back towards him), was riding round to every
nearby farmhouse asking everyone to come at
once and to bring all the food they had in
their larder for the biggest picnic in history.

They weren't at all keen. There were still a
number of people who thought the giant
should be murdered while he slept. There were
even more who thought the king and queen –
or Florizella and Bennett – should move him
on without delay. But Florizella, who could be
very persuasive when she tried, told them all

that the only way they would get rid of the giant for good, would be to feed him up, to equip him with spectacles and seeds, and then send him home. "We have to help him look after himself," she said. "Besides, he doesn't mean any harm. He's only little."

How Florizella could call a twenty-metre giant "little" was beyond most people. But the nicer people felt sorry for Simon. And the crosser ones were not going to attack him on their own. So Florizella got her way and very soon led them all, in wagons and farm-carts, coaches and carriages, to the wood on the Plain Green Plains where the giant was obediently sitting, as still as he could.

They built great bonfires, they roasted oxen on spits as big as trees. They piled mound upon mound of bread-dough into bath-tubs and set them to cook on the hot embers. They baked a thousand potatoes in the hot ashes, they trailed string after string of sausages like bunting through the flames where they cooked and spat and sizzled. They fetched a big empty swimming-pool from somewhere and threw into it lettuces by the hundred, tomatoes by the thousand, and lorry-loads of onions for a fresh salad.

"Not *more* onions!" Florizella said.

They went to a garden centre and bought the biggest ornamental fishpond that anyone had ever seen, with a lovely circular wavy edge, and into it they poured all the milk from the dairy, all the custard powder they could lay their hands on, stirred it up, and then poured a long stream of red jelly on top. When it had set, which took several hours, they called out the Seven Kingdoms' World Famous Weight-Lifting Team.

Dressed only in their smart blue trunks, their great muscles bulging with the strain, the twenty strong men stood on one side of the enormous jelly mould. At the count of three they tipped it up, slowly, slowly, slowly, until it was on its side and then crashed down on to a sheet of corrugated iron which was to be the giant's pudding plate.

They stepped back, bowed at the crowd and slapped each other on the back. That was the first stage completed. The second stage was even harder. They all stood round the upside-down jelly mould and gripped the rim. They heaved and heaved and heaved, while their muscles bulged and their eyes popped out and their faces went most dreadfully red. There was an exciting moment when nothing happened, and then with a great...

Flubb

the biggest jelly-and-custard trifle in the
world slithered out of the jelly mould and
sat wobbling temptingly in the sunlight like
a small red and yellow island.

When it was all ready, two hundred sea
scouts from the Seven Kingdoms' Navy came
struggling up with a great sail from a tall-
masted sailing ship. Carefully they spread it
out, heaved it up on to the giant's knees and
heaped all the food on it.

Then the giant, using his huge fat fingers, very carefully picked up all the potatoes, sausages, bread, roasted oxen and salad and ate and ate and ate. He used a scoop from a bulldozer to eat the trifle. In his hand it was like a dainty little teaspoon. He dug into the jelly-and-custard island for shovel after shovel until finally it was all gone.

Every delicious slurpy bit.

It was unbelievable how much he ate. Florizella and Bennett watched in amazement as all the food which they had gathered from the length and breadth of the kingdom disappeared. Samson kept a keen look-out for leftovers. He was starting to like the giant.

"Have you had enough?" Florizella yelled up at him. She was perched on one of his knees, clinging to his "tablecloth".

The giant beamed down at her.

"That was grand! What is for tea?"

"We'll think about tea later," Florizella said firmly. "I want you to wait here now, while we see if we can help you with your eyesight."

"Sit still again?" Simon asked. He was disappointed.

"Yes!" Florizella shouted at him.

"I thought friends played games together. I thought the three of us might play a game."

"I have to find my parents," Florizella said quickly. "They will be wanting to meet you."

"Can't we have a quick game before you go? What about hide-and-seek?"

Florizella gazed up at the enormous giant. Even sitting down, his head poked high above the tops of small trees. Standing up, he was taller than the wood. The only place he would ever be able to hide would be among the highest of mountains. And then his boots would fill a small valley.

"We'll play something later," Florizella promised. "Will you sit still now?"

Simon was reluctant.

"Isn't there anyone who will play with me? Or even talk to me? I'd like someone to tell me a story."

Florizella looked. Everyone who had been standing round doing nothing and listening to Florizella talking to the giant suddenly became tremendously busy and had no time at all.

Everyone, except one little girl.

She came up to Florizella and smiled a wide, gap-toothed smile. She nodded her curly head. "I'll talk to him," she said to Florizella. " I think he'th thweet."

Florizella looked doubtfully at her. She was such a small girl, dressed in a blue pinafore dress with very clean white socks and blue shoes with little straps.

"How old are you?" Florizella asked.

"Thix," the little girl said. "I could tell him thtorieth."

Bennett gave a giggle and turned it into a cough. The little girl was not fooled. She looked at him severely.

"There ith no need to thnigger," she said warningly. "I know thome very nithe thtorieth."

Florizella grinned. "What's your name?" she asked.

"Thethelia," the little girl said. "That'th unfortunate at the moment, becauthe I have a lithp while my front tooth ith growing."

"Oh! So you have!" Florizella said, kindly pretending that she had not noticed and scowling at Bennett who stuffed his fist into his mouth to muffle his laughter and ducked behind some trees.

Florizella called up to the giant. "There's a little girl down here called Cecilia. She says she'll tell you stories."

The giant lowered his great hand and Cecilia clambered into his warm, damp palm. Florizella watched as the giant raised her up to his eye level.

"Now," she heard her say. "I'll tell you all about Thleeping Beauty."

Chapter 5

The king and queen, who had taken a good long time to get the royal court moving, just as Florizella had predicted, were actually only an hour away from the giant when Florizella and Bennett met them on the road. With the royal procession was the royal zoo keeper, the royal surveyor, the royal enchanter, two hundred of the royal guard and about a hundred other people who had nothing better to do on a fine summer's day than to come along and see what was happening.

"Hullo Florizella!" the king said, as Florizella came cantering up on Jellybean. "Found the giant?"

"Yes!" Florizella said in a rush. "He's only young and he's short-sighted and lonely. But he *will* go back to his own country if we can help him to plant his vegetable garden."

The king blinked a bit. "Oh good," he said. He smiled at the queen. "Looks like Florizella has it all under control," he said. "Perhaps we should go home and leave it all to her."

The queen smiled. "I'll just see this giant

before we go," she said. "Sometimes Florizella's ideas get a little out of hand."

"How do you make spectacles?" Florizella interrupted.

"I expect I could magic a little something," the royal enchanter offered grandly.

"Go on then," Florizella said.

There was a small clap of thunder and a puff of green smoke and in the road before them stood the most amazing scene. There were dancing girls with ostrich feathers in their hair, there were elephants, there were fireworks exploding brightly in the sky, there were trapeze artists, there was a railway train painted in gold with a song-and-dance rag-time band on silver wagons behind it, there were dancing bears, there were acrobats, there were jugglers, there were fountains pouring into silver basins, there were rose petals tumbling down in scented showers from out of the thin air.

"No, no," Florizella said crossly. "I meant a pair of spectacles."

The royal enchanter waved his wand again.

There was another small explosion and at
once there was a huge Ferris wheel with
dancing girls waving and singing from the
swinging chairs, a showboat paddling its way
up the chalky road with people tap-dancing
on the top deck, and a flying circus high in
the sky with beautiful girls and handsome

men standing on the wings of little bi-planes
which trailed coloured smoke and flags.
There was a brass band, a troupe of clowns,
a magician pulling out of every pocket
coloured doves, which flew around in circling
flocks, and about a hundred milk-white
horses cantering round a circus ring.

"No! No!" Florizella said. "A pair of spectacles to help someone who is short-sighted."

"Oh, sorry," the royal enchanter said. With a puff of blue smoke the whole thing disappeared as suddenly as it had come.

"I say, Florizella, that looked rather fun," the king said wistfully.

"I need spectacles for the giant," Florizella said. "He is most dreadfully short-sighted, and until he can see properly he cannot go back to his own land and plant his own garden."

"I can't do that sort. It's a bit scientific for me," the royal enchanter said.

"Is it possible to make spectacles big enough to fit a giant?" Florizella asked.

"I don't see why not," the royal surveyor offered. "It's just a question of making ordinary spectacles only ten times bigger."

"Can we do it?" Bennett asked.

The royal surveyor took a gold pencil from behind his ear and a piece of paper from his pocket and started doing sums for a long time, whistling softly to himself while he worked.

"If everyone in the Seven Kingdoms donated a window from every household we would have enough glass," he said after a long while.

He held up his hand for silence and did his sums again. "If everyone donated a bit of their garden gates we would have enough metal for the frames," he said.

He did some more sums. "If we emptied one of the small pools at the edge of the Great Valley lake, and then filled it with all the window panes, and then made an enormous bonfire with all the wood from Bear Forest on top and set fire to it, keeping it stoked up all the time, we could melt the glass and the melted glass would form into the right sort of shape for lenses for spectacles."

The king and the queen gaped. "Burn the wood from Bear Forest?" they asked. "Empty the pools at the edge of Great Valley Lake?"

"Great Valley Lake is empty already," Bennett said apologetically. "We made it into lemonade and he drank it. Sorry."

"This *is* an emergency," Florizella said. "If he can't see to plant his seeds he can't look after himself. If he can't find his way home we'll never get rid of him. And everyone called him stupid at school which isn't fair. And he *is* awfully nice."

"Oh, very well," the King said. "Send out a royal proclamation. But people aren't going to like it."

Chapter 6

In fact, people did not mind so very much. It is a rule in the Seven Kingdoms that anything you do not need is collected and shared. Empty bottles are washed and reused. Cardboard and paper is collected and mashed up and made into new paper. Even potato peelings and bits of vegetables and food are collected and fed to the herds of pigs, cows, and horses. If someone has a bicycle they don't use, they just paint it yellow and leave it outside their door. When someone else wants a ride they take it, and then leave it outside *their* door. Once people got the idea that there were plenty of bicycles around, they forgot all about stealing them and keeping them for their own. So the suggestion that since the whole kingdom had a problem with the giant, the whole kingdom had to do something about it, was not a great shock. Everyone saw at once that one window each was a small price to pay to get rid of the giant. And anyway, the summer was very fine with no rain, so they did not miss their windows as much as they would have done if it had been winter.

Everyone who had fancy iron gates cut the knobs and twiddly bits off the top and brought them to a great heap of scrap iron beside the royal camp on the Plain Green Plains. They were sorry for the short-sighted giant; but more than anything else they all hoped that the plan to make him spectacles would work, so that he could go home and grow his own crops, instead of eating so much of the food belonging to the Land of the Seven Kingdoms.

If the Seven Kingdoms had been an ordinary kind of place there would have been loads of broken bottles and scrap iron anyway. But for years they had only made exactly what they needed, and no more. "Which is all very well under ordinary circumstances," the king said crossly. "But when you have a giant arriving for an indefinite stay you like to have a bit of surplus."

The royal surveyor had surveyed the dry

bottom of the pool at the edge of Great Valley Lake.

"It's perfect," he said. "The glass in spectacles helps people to see because it is made slightly curved. The picture of the outside world is bent by the glass before the eye even sees it. The bottom of the lake is exactly the right curve. When the glass is melted by the fire and then cools and sets hard it will be exactly the right curve for the giant's eyesight."

All the members of the court and the royal guard and the people of the Plain Green Plains piled half the window panes into the lake, and half the wood on top. Then they lit the wood and let it burn and burn for two whole days and nights. All the children from Great Valley Lake School took another couple of days off without asking and had a barbecue round the lakeside which went on for two and a half days.

They had never had a summer like it.

After two days and two nights the fires burned down and the glass, which had melted under the heat, started to set solid again in the shape of the pool – flat on top and perfectly smoothly curved on the bottom. When the royal surveyor brushed the grey wood ash away, all the glass had melted into a smooth surface like ice on a pond.

Very carefully, without breaking it, they levered the glass from the bed of the pool and laid it on the soft grass of the Plain Green Plains. Then they put in the rest of the window panes and melted them too. All the children from Great Valley School took another couple of days off without permission. When they had finished they had two giant lenses for spectacles so big and so thick that it took four men to carry each one.

All that was left to do *then*, was for all the nearby blacksmiths to come with their forges, and heat and hammer all the twiddly bits from the fancy garden gates into a smart but simple pair of frames for the spectacles. Six blacksmiths rolled up in their blackened and dirty wagons and put all their forges together to make one really big hot fire. And all the blacksmiths' sons – who also should have been in school – puffed on the bellows and made the charcoal of the forges glow a bright and brilliant red. Then the blacksmiths took all the old scrap metal and hammered and bashed it, cooled it down and heated it up, twisted it and forged it, knotted it together and smoothed it out until...

"Done at last," said Princess Florizella with enormous relief.

It had been nearly a week since they had first met the giant and all that time Florizella had been riding Jellybean up to the lake, and back to the royal camp, off round the countryside to find more blacksmiths, to find more metal, and out every day to find more food for the giant.

That was the bit that Samson liked the best. He always sat beside the giant at mealtimes and he had never eaten so well in his life. Crumbs of bread and cake the size of boulders fell round him. Scraps of meat pies or cheese as big as cartwheels came tumbling down. Samson the wolf cub was the only one in the whole kingdom who was enjoying the giant's stay. He thought Giant Simon was just wonderful.

Once a day Bennett sounded a horn and the whole area for a kilometre round the giant was cleared of every person and every animal so that he could stand up and stretch. Only Cecilia stayed with him while he moved about. He had a little pocket in his shirt and he tucked Cecilia inside, to keep her safe.

"Aren't you at all nervous with him?" Bennett asked her. She was, after all, such a very little girl.

"Thilly," she said scornfully. "He ith an abtholute thweety-pie."

Bennett had to cough and go behind a tree again. But Florizella's mind was on the spectacles, which were rumbling towards them on a specially-built wagon drawn by six big plough-horses. Trailing a plume of chalky white dust behind it, the wagon came down the road towards the giant.

"I think I can see it!" the giant called. "I think I can see the wagon coming! I see a white blob coming along the road!"

"Hold still! Hold still!" Florizella shrieked as the giant boots stamped the ground in excitement. "Stand still, Giant Simon!"

The giant obediently froze – but if you looked upwards you could see his thick green-socked knees trembling with excitement.

"I think I can see my spectacles!" he said as quietly as he could manage. "On a big cart. Are they really going to make me see everything clearly?"

"Yes!" Florizella said, with her fingers crossed behind her back for luck.

"And then you can go home and plant your own food," Bennett reminded him.

"And no one will ever call you stupid again," Florizella said encouragingly.

The wagon drew to a standstill at the

giant's feet. Simon bent down very carefully. He put Cecilia on the ground beside Florizella and Bennett and then he picked up the spectacles by the frames and looked at them.

"Put them carefully on your nose," Florizella urged.

There was a long exciting silence while the giant settled them on his nose, pushed the arms of the spectacles into his curly fair hair, and tucked them behind his huge ears.

He gazed out across the Plain Green Plains. "I can see!" he said softly. "I can see properly at last. It's lovely. I can see the hills and the mountains behind them. I can see the trees."

He turned his big face to look downwards. "And I can see my friends..." he started softly...

Then he screamed in absolute terror – so loudly that Florizella, Bennett, Cecilia and all the royal court were blown over and over by the blast...

"Humans! Humans! Ugh! Humans! I hate humans! I thought you were mice!"

"Stand still! Stand still!" Florizella and Bennett yelled, as the giant tried clumsily to jump away from the royal camp while the king and queen and the royal surveyor and the whole court clung to bushes and trees as the whole world shook round them. "You'll hurt us! Stand still!"

The plough-horses threw up their heads and bolted in six different directions at once. Their driver leaped clear of the wagon, which overturned and was dragged zigzagging wildly away. People ran screaming with terror as the mighty boots crashed down first in one spot and then in another, like great unpredictable thunderbolts. High, high above them, above the tops of the trees, they could hear the roaring complaints of the frightened giant.

"I hate humans! I hate humans! They're 'orrible! 'orrible! I hate them. They're dangerous! They're nasty! They're sneaky! They come after you when you ain't done nothing! 'orrible! 'orrible!"

"Stand still!" Florizella yelled. "Stand still and listen for a moment!"

The giant forced himself to stand still, quivering all over with fright.

"We're not 'orrible," Florizella said. "I mean horrible. We've been kind to you – remember? We've made you these spectacles and it took all the glass we had and all the iron! We've fed you every day! We're not sneaky and nasty!"

The giant shook his head. He was hopelessly confused.

"Cecilia is a human," Florizella gabbled at the top of her voice. "And you like her. She tells you wonderful stories. And you like Bennett – he brought you lemonade when you were thirsty. And you like me – and all of us here. We've fed you for a week. We've cared for you."

The giant shook his head.

"I don't believe you! I've heard all about you! It was one of your tricks – being nice to me. I know all about humans! You'd have tied me up when I was asleep or something sneaky like that! You'd have come climbing up beanstalks after me! You'd steal my gold or set other giants on me! Well, you watch out, Princess Florizella! Fee-fi-fo-fum you know! I am a giant after all! I can grind your bones don't forget!

Fee-fi-fo-fum!
Fee-fi-fo-fum!

I can't remember how the rest of it goes ... Umpty umpty umpty um!"

He finished the last "umpty-umpty-umpty-um!" with a great roar, trying very hard to hide his own fear and to frighten everyone else.

"What are we going to do?" Florizella demanded of Bennett in an urgent whisper. "If he goes on about grinding bones the royal guard won't like it at all! And then we'll have a little war on our hands."

"A giant war you mean," Bennett said. "And *we've* given him spectacles so he can see us. We won't have a chance if he attacks!"

Florizella looked behind her. Already people were getting up and looking for weapons, and grouping round the king and queen. They all looked angry and frightened. The royal guard gathered to the royal standard with their hands on their swords. The drummer girls were looking for their drum sticks in a hurry in case anyone wanted to sound the retreat – or even advance. The queen beckoned urgently to Florizella to come to her. Florizella smiled pleasantly and waved back, pretending not to understand.

Suddenly Cecilia, the very little girl, pushed between Florizella and Bennett.

"Lift me up!" she demanded. "Lift me up on your shoulder."

Bennett picked her up. She was still only as high as the giant's laces on his monstrous boots.

"Thimon!" she yelled. "Giant Thimon! Can you hear me?"

The giant stopped still at her commanding little squeak. "Yes," he said a little more softly. "I can hear you, Thethelia."

"You are a big thilly to thpeak to Florithella like that," she said severely. "She hath been ath nithe ath she could be. And then you thtart up with thith fee-fi-fo-fum nonthenth.

You should be ashamed
of yourthelf. You are a
great big naughty thing."
"I..." the giant began,
but it was no use.
Cecilia was quite
unstoppable.
"Now, you thay
thorry," she said
firmly. "Or no
one ith going to
talk to you."
There was a
long silence.
"THAY THORRY!"
Cecilia shouted
with infinite
threat.

"Thorry," the giant said. "I mean, sorry. I was startled. I've never talked with humans before. I thought you were all horrid little vermin that climb up beansprouts to steal money and murder innocent giants. A race of burglars and killers. I thought you were all called Jack."

"That's just a fairy story," Florizella said.

"Sorry," the giant said more softly. "I thought it was true. I thought we were natural enemies."

Bennett shook his head. "There are no natural enemies," he said. "You can always be friends if you choose to be. We'd like to be friends with you."

The giant shuffled his feet, rather dangerously.

"I'm sorry," he said again very humbly. "I want to be friends. I was very frightened for a moment, that was all."

"That'th better," Cecilia said firmly.

The giant bent down and put out his big warm hand. The three children climbed into it. He lifted them up and up and up, past the tree trunks, past the high branches of the trees, past the birds' nests and the tops of the trees, up to his face.

His big blue eyes were huge behind his new specs, as big as two blue harvest moons. The effect was quite startling: Florizella found she was gazing and gazing into his deep, enormous eyes.

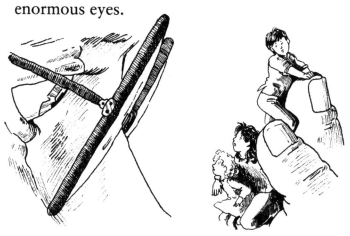

"I *am* sorry," he said again. "I know you're nice now. But I was always taught that humans were dreadful."

"There are good and bad," Cecilia said. "Jutht like giantth, jutht like all people."

Florizella and Bennett exchanged an amazed look.

"This Cecilia is one smart little girl," Bennett whispered to Florizella. Aloud he said, "If you are ready to leave, Giant Simon, then we have some vegetables and seeds and plants for you." He pointed towards the horizon where there was a long train of carts loaded high with sacks of tomato seeds, lettuce seeds, carrot seeds, potato seeds, marrow seeds, cucumber seeds, corn on the cob seeds, parsnip seeds, and behind them more wagons piled high with little fruit trees, their branches tossing with the rolling of the carts along the road.

The giant gave a little sigh of pleasure. The three children grabbed on to his thumb and no one was blown away.

"That's a wonderful sight," he said. "It's very kind of you all. I shall take them and plant them and my garden will be the best of all gardens. And then I shall have friends who will come round to see it. They won't call me stupid then! They'll be pleased to know me!"

He bent down and put the children softly on the ground. With delicate fingers he picked the tiny vegetables out of the carts and looked at them carefully. He could see them properly at last. "These are grand!" he said. "Grand. I'm very very grateful to you all."

"It's our pleasure," the king said graciously. "And now I think it is probably time for you to go, Giant Simon."

It was a little unfortunate that everyone nodded very enthusiastically at the prospect of the giant leaving.

"We will be sorry to lose you," the queen said tactfully. "But I expect you will want to be getting back to your garden. Autumn is coming, you will want to be getting the ground ready for your crops."

"We'll point you in the direction of your home," Bennett said. "You came from the west, from over the mountains."

The giant had gone very quiet .

"We'll send the wagons along behind you," Florizella said cheerfully. "They can follow you until they reach our borders, and then you can carry the seeds and trees to your home."

The giant said nothing. He sighed deeply. All the flags at the royal camp streamed out in the wind of his sigh. A few tents blew over.

"Watch out," Bennett said to Florizella. "I think he's getting tearful!"

A fat solitary tear crashed down into the bushes beside the two children, like a single massive wave on a beach.

"Don't cry!" Florizella yelled desperately. "What's the matter?"

"Hold the horses!" Bennett shouted to the royal camp. "Fasten down the tents! Prepare for a storm!"

"Unh-hunh!"

The ground rocked with the giant's sob.

"Unh-hunh! Unh-hunh!"

"What *is* it?" Florizella shouted upwards.

"I'm going to miss you!"

The giant was bawling like a baby.

"I'm going to have to go back to my own country all by myself, and no one will tell me stories there."

Tears cascaded down upon the children and the royal camp like a hurricane, like a typhoon. The giant's sobs uprooted great trees, a tent was washed away, several flagpoles were snapped off, the banners swept away on the gale of his cries.

High above the noise a little voice was raised. "Thtop it!" said Cecilia indignantly. "A great big giant like you! You should be ashamed of yourthelf!"

Abruptly the giant stopped crying.

"You are too big to be thquealing and

thnivelling all the time," Cecilia said firmly.
"Bethideth, there ith no need for it. I am
coming back with you to your country. I have
athked my mum and she thayth I can. We can
plant your garden together. I will thtay with
you till the end of the thummer holidayth.
And Florithella and Bennett will vithit you
when you are thettled again."

"Will you?" the giant asked. "Will
you come with me, Thethelia? Stay
with me until the end of the summer?
And will you visit me, Florizella and
Bennett?"

The children shouted, "Yes, of course! Of
course we will!" and watched anxiously as
the giant wiped the last tears from his eyes
with the back of his hand.

"I tell you what! We'll have a party to see
you off!" the king shouted up. "I expect
you'd like some fireworks wouldn't you?
A nice jolly farewell party?"

"With hats?" Giant Simon asked eagerly.
"And things that you blow that

squeal? And streamers? And games?"

Florizella and Bennett looked reproachfully at the king. "Oh Daddy, look what you've done," Florizella said reproachfully. "How on *earth* are we going to make him a party hat? Or a blower?"

"Sorry," the king said. "I was just thinking of the royal enchanter's spectacular show."

"Oh, yes!" Florizella said delightedly. "It's not like any party you've ever seen before!" she yelled up at the giant. "No hats, but the most wonderful things! You just wait till you see it!"

The royal enchanter stepped forward. His magic blue coat billowed round him, his tall pointy hat was slightly askew. "An amusing little something?" he asked the king with a smile.

"Something for the children," the king said. "They've been so good!"

The royal enchanter produced a long silvery wand from his drooping sleeve and tapped it lightly on the ground. At once a white marble fountain sprang out of the ground, bubbling and flowing with raspberry soda. Fireworks leaped out of the grass and whizzed up into the evening sky, popping and twinkling in a million different colours. The showboat which had so caught the king's fancy earlier, came pounding up the road with its paddles turning and very loud music and dancing on the top deck. A dozen incredibly fast, incredibly slippery waterslides appeared from nowhere and the children from the Great Valley Lake School (*never* had they had such a summer!) dashed for them and flung themselves, still fully dressed, up the steps and then screaming, round and round, head over heels, down the waterslides. A little steam engine with carriages came chuffing up the road and high-kicking dancing girls wrapped in feather boas sprang out of every door and danced up and down. A thousand parachutes opened in the sky above them and a regimental brass band floated lightly down playing ragtime jazz, never missing a note, even when they dropped to the ground and

rolled. High on the crest of a billowing blue wave, a dozen world-class surfers came dipping and wheeling, riding the high plumes of sea spray through the little forest.

"Now *that's* what I call a spectacle!" the royal enchanter said to the royal surveyor with a superior sort of smile.

But Florizella had something on her mind. She looked round the crowd of laughing delighted faces until she saw Cecilia's mother. She was laughing and pointing at a circus which had just arrived. There were unicorns doing a water ballet in rainbow-coloured water, with flying horses dipping and wheeling round rose-pink fountains.

"I say," Florizella asked. "Is it really all right for Cecilia to go with the giant?"

"Oh, yes," she said with a smile. "She's always been a great one for pets has Cecilia. She'll stay till he's settled in and then she'll come home again. I let her go away for the holidays as long as she is back in time for school."

"Pets?" Florizella asked. "Does Cecilia call Giant Simon a pet?"

"Oh, yes," the woman said. "Now all my children want one."

Florizella shook her head. "I just hope it doesn't become a craze," she said. "I don't think we can manage more than one a year!"

"Let them go, Florizella," Bennett said. "If she has decided that Giant Simon is her pet then she'll insist on keeping him. I'd rather she went with him than decided that she should keep him here. That is one little girl who gets her own way!" He cupped his hands round his mouth and shouted upwards. "Well, goodbye, Giant Simon. We'll come and see you in the autumn."

"Goodbye!"

the giant boomed down at them. Fireworks exploded behind his head and he laughed delightedly.

"Goodbye everyone, and thank you for everything, especially the party!"

"Tho long!" Cecilia called from high up in the giant's pocket. "I'll be home in time for thchool in the autumn!"

The huge giant and the little girl in his pocket waved to the royal court and to Princess Florizella and Prince Bennett and then, with the wagons of seeds and trees following behind him, the giant turned westward into the pale apricot evening sunlight and carefully stepped his way home, treading on nothing, stumbling into nothing, watching where he put his huge feet, and looking with pleasure all round him. As he walked, everyone could hear the piping voice of Cecilia going on and on and on with her unending stories.

Everyone watched him until he was a long way off, treading carefully along the white track of the road as if it were a chalk line

drawn for a game. The fireworks and the
rockets and the parachuting band and the
showboat and the train and the circus
followed him into the distance and then faded
from sight as a dream trickles away when you
wake. When the giant was nothing more than
a small moving dot on the horizon everyone
breathed a sigh of relief and started packing
up the royal camp.

"I rather liked him," Florizella said. "I'm glad we were able to make spectacles for him."

"And give him his seeds and his trees," Bennett said. "We could ride over to fetch Cecilia at the end of the summer holidays, and see how his garden is getting on."

"It was a good adventure," Florizella said.

"Yes," Prince Bennett replied. "Well done, Florithella."

"Thuper," she said with a grin.